AN INNOCENT'S DIARY

ROHAN M. BHOSALE

Copyright © Rohan M. Bhosale
All Rights Reserved.

This book has been published with all efforts taken to make the material error-free after the consent of the author. However, the author and the publisher do not assume and hereby disclaim any liability to any party for any loss, damage, or disruption caused by errors or omissions, whether such errors or omissions result from negligence, accident, or any other cause.

While every effort has been made to avoid any mistake or omission, this publication is being sold on the condition and understanding that neither the author nor the publishers or printers would be liable in any manner to any person by reason of any mistake or omission in this publication or for any action taken or omitted to be taken or advice rendered or accepted on the basis of this work. For any defect in printing or binding the publishers will be liable only to replace the defective copy by another copy of this work then available.

To my parents, Mr. Mahendra Bhosale and Mrs. Rekha Bhosale

My entire world revolves around you.

You are the light in my life.

You are my love and my entire life

The thing that completes my soul.

To all the hopless Romantics and to myself.

And to all the girls looking for the prince but fall for the bad guy.

Contents

Preface

An Innocent's Diary is a book very to my hear, being my debut novel. Though none of the events described are true, I have a very emotional and sentimental attachment with the story.

It was back in 2021 when I felt like writing a novel of my own. I was sitting with a very dear friend of mine speaking about books and then i just told her that I have an idea, a story do you want to listen? I told her a brief story which was going on my mind. she was the one who gave me the idea to bring this fictional world on paper and told me to publish it. Well then characters were developed, scenes were set and emotions were printed and I sucessfully wrote the novel. So basically I can say that the inspiration of this novel is this friend of mine. Without her support this fiction would've never been brought infront of the world on paper.

I have a very special connections with writings of specific writers like the sad scenes described by John Green, the romance potrayed by Colleen Hoover and the sensual spice potrayed by the writings of Anna Todd. So likewise, their work also inspired me to write this novel.

So please take your time and read the novel that has effforts of many people behind it and my blood, sweat and tears.

- Love, Rohan Bhosale
THE AUTHOR.

Prologue

He was just an ordinary young man, broken by the world and potrayed as a villain. He was the innocent but yet was tagged as guilty.

She was the one to see his pain and endure it, heal his wounds of hatred with the bandages of her love.

A hero will sacrifice her and save the world to show that he is indeed pure hearted but the villain would tear apart the world if she's hurt and that is his promise. A villain is selfish, manupalative and rude to everyone but he will treat her like a queen , his and only his, sitting with him on a throne with her crown. a villain is often misjudged in the story. But this story is about the misjudged. It is said that all good guys go to heaven but Bad boys bring Heaven to you.

Epigraph

"My thoughts are stars I cannot fathom into constellations."
- From 'The Fault In Our Stars' by John Green.

List Of Characters

1. Reia: The teenage girl to embark this journey.
2. Om: Pale, lean and cute friend from second year
3. Neha: Reia's Childhood Friend.
4. Sanjana: Neha's elder sister.
5. Dhruv: Reia's classmate.
6. Sana: Reia's classmate.
7. Zain: Reia's classmate.
8. Mr Ansh Gupta: English Literature professor
9. Dr. Satyamurthy: Principal of IEC
10. Mr and Mrs Sharma: Reia's Mom and Dad
11. Sahil, Jay and Avantika: Om's friends
12. Devansh: A tall dark and muscular dude with the dark past.
13. Mr Shah: Devansh's dad

About The Author

Rohan Bhosale is a 2003 born, architecture student. The other side of him is a young budding writer fascinated by the world of fiction. He mostly works on Young Adult Romance-Fiction. He also loves to write poetry which can be explored on his instagram handle (provided below). An Innocent's Diary is his debut novel. Rohan is from Pune, India.

Where to find the author:

Facebook : Rohan Bhosale

Instagram : rohan_bhosale_24

Official Website : https://msha.ke/rohanbhosale

Disclaimer

This book is a work of fiction, it does not have any refrence to real world. The names of the characters are made up and not inspired from real life. If the name of any character resembles any name from the real world is a mere coincidencee.

ONE

A New Beginning.

Dear Diary, I'm excited for tomorrow, tomorrow is the first big chapter of my adult life. A new beginning after I turned 18. I'm going to college tomorrow. All the hard work I've done has finally paid off. I'm pretty excited for tomorrow, I have decided what dress to wear tomorrow, picked the matching earrings, a fancy pair of shoes. In the end, the first impression is very important. Well, it's past my bedtime so I should go to sleep now, got a big day tomorrow.

Then Reia stood up from the study table kept her diary in the cupboard and went to her bed, turned off the lights and fell asleep. The alarm started ringing when the hour hand reached 8 in the morning. She stretched her hand out of the blanket and turned off the alarm and went back to sleep.

Reia's mother came to wake her up after a couple of minutes, "Wake up darling it's 8, gotta get ready for the first day of your college." Reia slowly opened her hazel eyes, the ray of sunshine coming through the window beside her bed, lighting up her face leaving an eternal glow. A small and cute smile flashed on her face looking at her mother she said after a small yawn, "Yeah Ma, I'm up I'll get ready." "Get ready and come down in twenty minutes, I'll plate the breakfast", her mother said.

After some time she got up. She entered the bathroom took a bath and got out of the bathroom. She went to the wardrobe put her clothes on and sat on the chair in front of the dressing table brushing her luscious brown locks.

As she was walking downstairs in the cherry red dress that complemented her dark skin, with her flowing hair and her glowing face her parents were looking with shining eyes at their grown-up daughter who grew up so beautiful so quick. Reia came by the table and asks, "What's that smile of yours?"

Her father replied," You are the reason for our smile baby girl, it seems just like yesterday when we used to give you a shower, dress you up and then I used to carry you everywhere; and today we see a beautiful young lady walking up to us." Her dad's eyes filled with pride "Girl, you look straight fire" her mom said giggling (giving a reference to today's youths' slang) and then kissed her forehead. She sat on the table near her dad and ate her oatmeal.

Then there was a knock on the door. Reia went and opened the door. Her friend Neha wearing a yellow dress and her elder sister Sanjana wearing a red t-shirt and black jeans came to pick her up in a car. "Let's go Reia" said Neha as Reia opened the door. " Yeah, I'm ready I'll just take my bag and then let's hustle".

Neha was Reia's childhood friend. They both were together from preschool to High School. They were together in their joy and sorrow, through their ups and downs. Likewise, they were also gonna embark on this new journey together.

Then they left the house. Reia waved at her parents, her mother passed a flying kiss back. The trio (Reia, Neha and Sanjana) got in the car with Sanjana in the driver's seat and Reia and Neha in the back seat and headed to college, 'IEC Institute of Technology'. IEC was the most prestigious college in the State. Getting into that college was very crucial.

If you get in, it was a big deal. Each year over one lakh students used to fight for 108 prestigious seats. Both Reia and Neha put their blood, sweat and tears to get in and their reward was just a few minutes away. Reia and Neha were chit-chatting about how excited they are about college.

After a few kilometres they reached the gate of IEC, it was a huge iron gate opening half giving enough space for the car to get in. They reached the parking lot, parked the car and got out. Neha exclaimed, "I still can't believe that we are actually in THE 'IEC'!"

They approached the main college building. They stood stunned in front of the huge granite cladded building standing there for over 100 years but does not look a year old, with a huge wooden door opened by Sanjana leading Reia and Neha. Behind the doors, were hundreds of students going to their classes, picking up their books, fooling around etc.

After some time an announcement flashed, a deep manly voice addressing, "All the first-year students to please gather in the auditorium for the induction programme. The programme will begin at sharp 10 AM." Reia and Neha headed towards the auditorium along with the other first years'. Most of them trying to make new friends by communicating with each other. They all entered the auditorium. It was a very big auditorium wooden floored with cascade seating and a gallery too. It was literally like a movie theatre. There was a stage with a podium on it in front and a poster with 'Welcome the class of 24' written on it.

Reia and Neha climbed up a few stairs and found two vacant seats and sat near two other students. A black-haired girl sitting beside Neha offered her hand to Neha and said, "Hi, I am Sana, a pleasure to meet you". Neha smiled back at her and was about to speak when a guy sitting beside Sana offered his hand next and said, " And I am Dhruv." Then Neha said, "Pleasure to meet you guys, I'm Neha". And then Reia added " Hi Sana, hi Dhruv I'm Reia" and offered her hand. Sana shaking her hands with Reia said, "Hi Reia". And then Dhruv added, "Hi Reia pleasure to meet you too".

After some time the induction programme began with a welcome speech by a faculty member and then welcomed the Principal of the College, Dr Archana Satyamurthy. She was an old, sedate lady with a straight face (a typical head of the institute). She came up and said, " Welcome all to IEC, an institution that creates legends every year, a place where success is for sure. I congratulate you all for getting a seat in IEC through your sheer talent. These four years will be very tough but at the time very fruitful. You will make new friends but you may also lose some. Then she addressed the students about the rules and regulations of the institute and wished them luck for the future.

The programme ended with a gratitude note. After the programme concluded, Dhruv said, "Let's go to the cafeteria." The four of them then headed to the cafeteria.

Reia was walking backwards facing the others behind her and speaking with Neha, Dhruv and Sana, "I'm really happy, I think I'm dreaming. I'm just excited for......" She collided with someone and fell into a guys arms (like a typical

Bollywood movie). As she was looking at him all stunned, her inner voice was, "Oh my goodness what a cute guy just caught me. He has such a sweet smile!". She stood up and apologised, "I am very sorry actually I was speaking with my friends and...... ". He interrupted her and said," No worries in fact I'm lucky that I was able to catch and protect such a beauty" on which Reia blushed. He added," I'm Om by the way, from Second Year and you?" and led his hand for a handshake.

Reia shook his hand and replied," I'm Reia from First Year"." Oh, so it's your first day here, so do you want to sit there at that table with my friends I'll introduce y'all to them?", Om replied. Reia agreed and shook her head with a smile. Neha added, "Yeah sure. It'll be good to know some seniors."

They reached the table occupied by three other seniors. Then Om started introducing his friends," This is Sahil (pointing towards a tall, dark guy), this is Pranay (a pale muscular dude) and that miss gorgeous over there is Avantika (pointing towards the curvy brunette beauty). And then introduced the juniors next, "Guys this is Reia, Sana, Neha and Dhruv". All of them spent their hour or so in the canteen hanging out with their seniors and getting to know them.

The college concluded and then Reia and Neha met Sanjana at the car and headed home.

In the car, Sanjana asked, " So how was your first day at IEC?" Neha replied, "Oh it was great, beyond our expectations. I enjoyed a lot. In fact, I think Reia enjoyed a more than me." "Who so?", asked Sanjana looking at Reia through the back mirror. Neha replied, " Cause she fell in arms of really cute senior". Reia added, "We'll it was an accident Sanjana". " Yeah when did I say it wasn't?", said

Sanjana. And both Neha and Sanjana started giggling.

Reia started thinking about Om while looking out of the window, the unplanned moment they shared in his arms, and started blushing and smiling to herself.

TWO

LOVE WAS IN THE AIR.

Dear Diary, college is going on really good. I've made a couple of new friends. The classes are going on great. I also befriended some seniors. I also met Om, he is also a senior. He is really cute, lean, pale and his curly hair adds to his cuteness and his smile is top-notch. I also accidentally fell in his arms. We spent a few days together and I am really enjoying his company. I like him or maybe I am in love with him. I don't know.

Reia then went to bed. The next morning Reia got ready and sat down at the dining table with her parents for breakfast. Her father asked, "So how is college going on bubba?" "It's going on great. The professors are really good. I've also made some friends. Till now it is going as I always dreamt", replied Reia.

" That's nice. Enjoy and cherish these days Reia, they will never come back. But yes it is also a crucial time where you will build your identity so simultaneously focus on your career too". Reia nodded her head in agreement.

"So what about boys Reia, how many guy friends you made huh?", asked her mother giggling. Reia replied smiling

"Mom!" "Right" her father said, "She is not ready for boys yet". Reia in an arguing voice said, " Dad! I'm 18 ok." Her dad said laughing, "So there is a guy then? "You guys are impossible", said Reia while leaving for college.

It was 9o clock. Reia entered the classroom for her lecture and sat with Dhruv. It was English Literature. English Literature was a subject that Reia specially opted for, cause she had a special place for literature in her heart. She enjoyed spending hours getting lost in the words that the authors wrote. Unlike, Neha hated to read so she didn't even think once about taking this class. It was the first English Literature lecture since college started. She was pretty excited about it. There was havoc in the classroom, students chit-chatting, goofing around.

The entire class became stone cold as the professor walked in. The professor was a young man not old more than 35 years, it was unusual cause most of the times literature professors are like old men or women who just look like have already been on their death bed.

The teacher was surprised to see such a huge number of students who took Literature. The professor said, "Well it's quite unusual to see a class full of students and that too for English Literature. I hope to see a class like this for the entire year". " If such a handsome teacher is gonna teach then I can ensure the strength of girls won't get outnumbered", a random girl shouted from behind. "Unfortunately, I'm married", replied the professor pointing at his engagement ring on which the class burst into laughter.

"Ok, ok quiet now," said the professor "Let me introduce myself, I'm Mr Ansh Gupta, I'm a graduate in Arts with English as my speciality and also I hold a PhD in English Literature that I completed from Harvard. So as this is your first class let's begin with a simple question, how many of y'all love to read?" On this almost everyone raised their hand including Reia and Dhruv.

"So what you read, which genre do you enjoy the most?", asked Mr Ansh pointing towards a boy. "Mostly science fiction", replied the boy. Ansh said, " Nice and what do you like about it the most, Mr......?" "My name is Zain" said the boy and continued "What I love the most about science fiction is how I am transported to a different world where humankind is on the verge of development. The awesome gadgets they describe and all". "Good, Zain", complemented Ansh.

"And what about you what do you read?" asked Mr Ansh to the girl sitting on the firstbench.Likewise he asked two-three more students and then came towards Reia. "And you miss back there in the purple shirt, what you like?", asked Mr Ansh to Reia. Reia answered, "I like to read romance novels". "Great and what specifically you like about it?"

And as she was about to answer entered a guy, tall, dark and lean dressed in all black top to bottom and wearing rugged combat boots. He entered and approached the backbench and sat down. Reia continued, "I like how beautifully author describes love, in words that we never can. The tension of love that author describes that makes you feel dreamy and want to just get lost into it. "Wow! what a description", exclaimed Mr Ansh, " And what's your name?" "Reia Shah" she replied.

"Great and what about you mister got a bit late did we?" asked in sarcasm to the boy in the back. "What's your name?" he asked. "Devansh" the boy replied. "So Mr Devash, what are your thoughts about romance novels? Have you read any romance?", asked Mr Ansh. Devansh replied, "Yes sir". "Can you name a few?" Me. Ansh asked. "Pride and

Prejudice, Lady Chatterley's Lover, Five Point Someone, etc", Devansh said. "Oh the classics!", exclaimed Ansh " So what do you think about them?"

"It's a waste of time" replied Devansh "It is something that can never be found in reality. All of the novels claim that true love is real that it is the centre of the universe." "And you don't think so?", asked Mr Ansh. Devansh answered, "No I don't think it's real. Love is fictional only found in mere pages of novels. From Fitzwilliam to Noah all are fools. There will never be Darcy finding his Bennett in the real world. People who think they will are just fools."

On this Reia felt offended and turned back and answered back angrily, "We'll it can be finding a woman as good as Elizabeth Bennett is not a lay man's job. And yes certainly a jerk like you will never find one". As Reia spoke the period bell rang and Mr Ansh said cooling the rising temper, " Alright class I think it is enough for today. Let's continue in the next lecture".

Reia packed her bag and looked back searching for Devansh but he was not there. Then Dhruv patted on Reia's arm and said, "Hey let us go Sana and others would be waiting for us in the cafe". Reia still looking for Devansh said, "Yeah let's go".

The two met Sana and Neha who were waiting for them outside the cafeteria, Dhruv said, " You guys won't believe what happened. The literature class was really good, it was full of drama". "What?", asked Neha. Dhruv answered, "Reia had a very heated debate with a guy in the class. Both of them arguing was very entertaining." Sana said smiling, "Well should've taken Literature man".

"It is not funny guys that guy is a jerk. He walked in late in the class and didn't even bother to ask and was really annoying".

Meanwhile, Om came with the others and kept a hand on Reia's shoulder and said, "Let's proceed, shall we?" Reia nodded with butterflies in her stomach just by feeling his arm on her shoulder. They reached the table and sat down with Reia and Om near each other, Dhruv and Sanjana opposite to them and Neha, Sana, Jay and Sahil adjacent to Dhruv. "So how was your day?", asked Jay to Sana. She replied, "Yeah it was ok, we were occupied the whole day didn't even get a chance to relax." "Well you will get used to it", replied Jay."And what about you Reia?"

Reia answered, "We'll it was going great until a bastard ruined it". "Why what happened?" asked Sanjana. "I got into an argument with a boy in the class."

"Well don't worry your mood will get better. I'm there to change it", said Om giving a side hug to Reia bringing her close to his chest. Reia was feeling a certain warmth an emotion she had never ever felt before. She was getting goosebumps as she heard his heart pound. She asked herself, " What is this that I am feeling is this what is called love?'"

THREE

It Was A Good Day.

Dear diary I'm very happy, I am going out with Om tomorrow. He said and I quote "Would you like to go out with me tomorrow? Like a date?" I was so freakishly happy that I was feeling to dance but held that thought back and said yes I'd love to. I really want the date to go well, I want that everything goes well tomorrow. I want us to work out. I'm really looking forward to tomorrow.

Reia barely slept last night. The excitement about the date kept her up all night. She woke up early and got ready. She wore a pink skirt with her hair tied up in a messy bun with curtain bangs. She wore a necklace that her grandma left for her. It was a beautiful pink sapphire stone shaped like a heart. The necklace had many good memories that Reia had with her grandma.

Reia came downstairs and sat near her mother on the couch and waited for Om. Her mother looked at her and exclaimed, "You are looking gorgeous Reia! I bet Om will be stunned just by looking at you. And that necklace of Grandma's is looking so good on you." And then her mom took some kajal that she applied and placed a dot behind Reia's ear (it is a tradition followed to protect anyone from a bad sight or evil). Reia was smiling at her mother, her happiness was clearly reflected by her smile and glow on her face.

The doorbell rang after a few minutes. Mrs Sharma (Reia's mother) stood up and opened the door. It was Om was standing with a pressed grey button-down tucked in black jeans. His hair quiffed up. He was holding a bouquet of fresh red roses in his right hand.

"Is Reia home? We planned to go out today", said Om. "And you must be Om", replied Mrs Sharma. Om answered, "Yes, I am indeed". Mrs Sharma said, "Reia, your date is here to pick you up."

Reia came to the door. Om was bedazzled the moment he saw Reia. He completely drowned in her beauty. He took a moment to come back and said with his cute smile, "Wow! yo- you look amazing Reia. Here this is for you". Om handed over the bouquet, offered his arm and said, " Shall we?" Reia's mother exclaimed, "Aren't you a gentleman!" Reia took his hand and headed out. Reia's mom said, "Enjoy your day guys and Om bring Reia back till 5 ok?" "Yes ma'am sure", said Om.

The couple headed to Om's car it was a white Sedan. Om opened the door for Reia and then got on the driver's seat. Om turned on the radio, 'First Love' by Forever Young started playing. Forever Young was an English boyband formed back in 2010.

Om was mumbling the lyrics of the song, when Reia asked, " You too listen to Forever Young?" "Yes", he replied, "Do you also listen to their work". Reia continued "Yeah, in fact, I fangirl them. I've been following them from the day they released their debut song, and still love them even though they disbanded". "Me too. And I still think they are the best boyband in the world to date.

Which is your favourite song?", Om asked. Reia replied, "All of their work is a masterpiece but Kiss Me is my vibe". Both of them kept on going about the band on their way to their destination.

After a while they stopped at a place called D' Gorment. Om got out of the car and opened the door for Reia. He offered her his hand and asked, "May I?" On which she blushed and with a smile and replied, "Why not" and gave her hand to Om. The moment her soft and delicate hand touched Om's strong and tough hands she immediately felt a spark, felt a rush of adrenaline. Then she came out of the car and they both headed towards the cafe. They approached table 7 that was booked in advance by Om. The table was cozy and with an romantic ambience, near the table was a window which displayed a beautiful shedding of autumn leaves.

Om pulled the chair for Reia to sit. And then went on and sat in front of her. Reia said, "This place is so beautiful, the ambience the mood. Everything here is memorable." On which Om added, "Alas I was worried if you would like it here?" On which Reia replied with a a hint of flirt, "I would like to go to any place as long as you are with me." "Oh Reia, I‘m flattered", Om replied teasing Reia. Both of them busted into laughter.

The waiter came near the table for the order. Om gave the order according to Reia's preference and also ordered one thing for her from his recommendation. He said, " One chicken sandwich and Red sauce mac for the lady and scrambled eggs for me and a love shot for both of us". Love shot was a speciality of cafe D' Gourment. It was a latte with a touch of hazelnut and a special ingredient which made it extra tasty and special.

The waiter returned with their order. And they started enjoy their meal. In the end they both took sip of the special love shot. Reia took only a sip and loved the latte, her face was saying it all. Om asked, "So how is it?" "It's amazing", Reia replied " It seems as if it is drink that's brewed in heaven. I'm in love with this". "And me?" Om asked.

On which Reia was surprised and happy. Her heart and brain screaming I LOVE YOU TOO but her mouth was lost words. There was a silence between them. Immediately a spotlight came directly on them and then an announcer announced, "It's karaoke time. And seems like we have our first couple who is gonna set the mood for us.

Om stood up and asked for Reia's hand and said, " Come on let's go". "No I can't sing, I'm a terrible singer", Reia said and refused to go. Om added, "I am terrible singer too ask my shower head" Reia giggled "But still I want to sing you know why because I want to sing with you and have a memory of us together."

Reia took Om's hand and walked up to stage. As they were walking the announcer said, "Here comes our first couple". What are your names?", asked the announcer? "I am Om", said Om and "I'm Reia", Reia added. "Give it up for Om and Reia!", announcer exclaimed followed by the applaud by audience.

Love in New York by Jason King and Elena Gonzalez started playing Om looked at Reia with a smile and then started singing his part and then Reia began nervously singing her part and started looking in Om's brown eyes and got lost in them and the song. They both enjoyed throughout the song and the song ended with a huge round of applause.

They both bowed at the audience and Om hugged Reia tightly. Reia had butterflies in her stomach her heart beating faster than normal. She also nervously wrapped her arms around him. Then they both returned to their table and sat down, with Reia leaning her head on shoulder and Om with his arms around her. They enjoyed a few songs by other couples and then headed out.

They both were walking towards car and Reia close to Om holding his arm tight. They reached the car and were standing by the car door with Reia's back towards the car door and Om right in front of her. Reia said, " Yes". Om was confused he didn't get why Reia said yes out of the blue.

Reia continued, Yes I am in love with you.' And pulled Om close to her she could hear Om's beating heart and Om could feel Reia's breath. They got really close just looking at each other, there was only a little room between them. Reia filled that gap by going close and kissed Om. His hand around her waist and pulled Reia on tip toes while she was holding his shirt's collar.

They stopped after a while and then Om kissed Reia's forehead and whispered in her ear, "I love you so so much." They got into the car and 'First Kiss' by Forever Young started playing.

Om dropped Reia at her home. Reia's mom opened the door and said, "Hope you guys had a good time?". "Yes Aunty", replied Om "See you tomorrow, Reia". Reia nodded and then Om left.

Reia closed the door and hugged her mom. "I think the day went really amazing." "Yes mom I'm really happy". "That's nice go freshen up your dad will come in a short while ten we will have dinner", said Reia's mother. Reia replied, "Yes mom" and went upstairs to her room.

Reia was really happy about what happened. She laid down on her bed thinking and blushing about the kiss. Her phone started ringing, it was Neha. She picked up the phone and Neha begun, "So how was your date R? Did he asked you? What you say? Tell me everything , no no just skip to the good part." Reid said laughing, "Cool, cool Neha. Yeah I had a wonderful time with Om today and yes he asked me". "What was your answer then? What you'd say?", asked Neha. "Mm... We kissed!", exclaimed Reia. Neha exclaimed in a complete awe, " OMG!" They spoke about it and then hanged up.

Reia had dinner and came upstairs and made her bed and laid down. She was thinking of Om and then her phone buzzed it was Om's text - "Had a great time with you Reia can't wait to see you tomorrow. I'll come to pick you up. Be ready. Love Om". Reia replied, "Me too and yeah I'll be waiting for you tomorrow at 8. Love you, bye good night". And Reia turned off the lights and went to bed.
The sun rose kissing Reia's face and leaving behind a golden glow on her face Reia's eyes opened up a little. She woke up

and looked at the clock it was 6 in the morning.

She woke up and got ready. At 7:30 she went down for breakfast. She had her breakfast and then heard a car honking. "It must be Om", said Reia "I better get going. Bye mum bye dad". She left steering giving her mom and dad a forehead kiss. "She looks happy doesn't she?", asked M Sharma to Mrs Sharma. "Yes she is and I am happy for her", she replied.

Reia and Om reached the college and departed for their classes after a tight hug. Reia headed towards Neha, Dhruv and Sana who were watching Reia from a distance and started teasing her as she came. On which Reia blushed and said, "Stop it and let's go or we will be late."

The day concluded and as per their daily tradition all of them headed towards the cafeteria.

Reia and the others sat down and Reia left a spot for Om beside her and started looking out for him. Om came from behind and hugged Reia tightly and kissed her cheek. "So how was your day?", asked Om. "Great and what about you?" "Well it concluded on a good note at least after I hugged you", he replied and sat down beside Reia. Sahil, Jay and Avantika joined them after a while. All of them ordered something to eat and we're chatting about how their day was. When Devansh entered the cafeteria and Dhruv said, "Hey look Reia your arch nemesis. That's the guy who debated with R." "He is kind of hot", said Sana.

When Dhruv looked at her on which she added, "Come on, how can you ignore that lean muscular frame and those amazing locks and plus the guy is wearing all black. Now that is kind of hot." On this Om said, "Yeah it's ok but I think you should stay away from him" looking towards Reia and then glanced at others and continued, "I mean you all he is not a good guy." "Why what happened?", asked Neha. "Just stay away", said Om.

Sahil interrupted and said, "Forget about that, are you guys excited for your Freshers' party?" "What when is Freshers?", Dhruv asked. " We all are planning it for a while now. So we decided to arrange it on this coming weekend at 'Ignite' club", said Om. "That's great I can't wait for the weekend", said Neha.
After hanging out for a few hours they all decided to leave. Om came up to Reia and said, " Can you go to home with Neha? Actually I am busy with the Freshers preparation and stuff." "Yeah yeah no problem I'll go with them", Reia replied. "Ok", said Om and hugged her " Text me when you reach and be ready tomorrow at 8." Reia nodded and left.

On their home with the others, Neha asked Avantika, "Hey do, why did Om said so about Devansh what happened with him?" Avantika answered, "Well Devansh, should be actually in third year but he was not able to complete his first year because he was behind bars for two years". " He went to prison!", Reia exclaimed. "Yes", Avantika said on which Neha added, "But why?" "He is charged for physically assaulting a girl from this institution." "Then how come he is out of the prison now?", asked Neha. "He was on a good behaviour so the Government gave him a chance and gave him bail till further decision", answered Avantika.

FOUR

MONSTER UNMASKED

'Dear diary, life is great. I'm doing good at college, I have great and supportive friends my parents love me and I also have a guy that immensely loves me. Om and I have spent a lot of time together now. I love everything about him, I love to be around him, I love his eyes, his curly hair and all of his smile for which I fell for at the beginning. Om also asked me to be my chaperone and partner at the Freshers' dance. I'm really happy and I thank God for this life'.

It was 8, Om reached at Reia's home and picked her up for college. Reia went for her lecture it was Coding class. She sat down and turned on the laptop and was set for class as the teacher was about to begun Devansh entered the class. The teacher spoke sarcastically, "Never on time, Mr Shah." Devansh grabbed a seat next to Reia. The class began and the teacher started teaching after a while the teacher noticed Devansh not paying attention and lost in his own world. The teacher asked him to leave the class. Devansh picked up all his belongings and left the class without any other word.

The day came to an end and Reia met Om at the college gate where he was leaving with some senior friends, Sahil and Jay weren't part of it. Reia waved at him and he ran to her and hugged her and lifted her up and kissed her.

She said, "Stop everyone is watching". "So let them. By the way I'm really looking forward for the Freshers' tomorrow", said Om. "Me too" replied Reia. "I'm going with those guys for tomorrow's preparation so I'll meet you tomorrow at 6 in the evening", said Om. " Yeah" Reia replied. And then they both left.

Finally came the day of Freshers', all the first year students were excited for the party. Reia got ready for the party. She wore a yellow dress that resembled a traditional ball gown but with a modern touch, her hair flowing without any hair bands and she wore her Grandma's necklace too. It was 5:45 Om reached Reia's house and knocked the door.

He was wearing a navy tux with a white buttoned shirt tucked in with navy trousers and a navy bow tie. He brought Reia a beautiful corsage for her. He took Reia's hand in his hand and wrapped the corsage around her wrist. "You're looking like a beautiful princess Reia and I can't believe that this princess is my date today. I think that I am dreaming", said Om and kissed Reia's hand. Then they both went to the car and headed towards Ignite.

The couple reached there and entered the club with holding arms together. The club guards opened the door to a big space with a centre stage decorated with a board stating 'Welcome aboard' with a soft violin playing in the background Reia went to meet Neha and Sana. Neha was accompanied to the dance by Dhruv and Sana by Jay. They all were chatting and then came up a senior dressed crisp wearing a black tuxedo. "Good evening Freshies, I am Mayank Shetty your host for today. So without further adieu should we start the party? ", he said. All the people screamed, "YES". "So let's start DJ drop the beat".

Upbeat hip hop music started and everyone started to unwind grooving on the dance floor. And then the intensity dropped and a slow romantic music started playing all the couples in each other's arms square dancing. Reia leaning on Om's chest enjoying the music played by Om's beating heart. Then the DJ again played a hip hop jam after a while.

Then everyone started to dance again with energy and enthusiasm.

Reia was tired she was dancing now for quite a while. She went and sat on a bench and noticed that Om wasn't there. A guy came and sit beside her holding a glass of punch. She looked at him and found out it was Devansh.

He was all alone in the party with no one to enjoy with and no one to speak with. So she decided to keep all the odds aside and speak with him, " Hey Devansh, how are you?" On which he stood up and walked away. At the exact moment, Om came up to Reia and offered a glass of punch. "Where were you?", asked Reia. "I was with the boys making some arrangement.", said Om. Reia said, "Oh okay" and took a sip from the punch.

After a few moments Om asked Reia to come with him. He said, "Hey Reia let's go I have to show you something. Something very special". Reia took Om's hand and went with him. He escorted her to the parking lot. She was feeling a bit dizzy, she thought she was tired because of all the dancing.

As they reached Om's car a guy held Reia from back and grabbed her waist, Reia startled and started to move to get lose from his grip when two other guys came up. Those were the guys with whom Om was hanging out lately. Om said, "Don't be afraid they are my friends. They just want some good time". They started to molest her grabbing her breast and touching in areas that weren't supposed to Reia was crying for help but no one could hear her. One grabbed the necklace she was wearing and pulled it a broke it.

A guy screamed, "Let her go" Om turned back to see who it was. The moment he turned someone smacked him on his face and knocked him down. Then he grabbed other guy and separated him from Reia and pushed him down on this the other guy retaliated and approached him and kicked the approaching boy right in the crotch. Reia fell down helpless. Her saviour fought bravely the three men and knocked them down. He gave Reia his hand to help her stand up. She took his hand and looked up right at him, it was Devansh.

He then gave her his leather jacket to cover up her exposed as the dress was torn. He didn't even glanced at her. He said, "You are safe now go to your friends and return back home. You are safe now."

A few days were passed after the incident happened. Reia told her family everything and a legal complaint was made and her father being a lawyer was trying his best so that those four bastards get the punishment for their crime. But all the four of them including Om we're MIA.

Reia took some time and came back to normal and continued her college routine. She came back to college with Neha and Sanjana. Everyone of her friends were comforting her. She did all the lectures and then wanted some fresh air. She went to the library.

She sat their for a while reading a book about Advancements in software. She saw Devansh sitting on a table a bit far. She was carrying his jacket which she wanted to return and also wanted to thank him for that day. So she went up to him and sat beside him and returned him his jacket and said, "Here is your jacket Devansh and I can never thank you enough for saving me the that day. If you wouldn't have saved me then I can't imagine what they would've done to me. Thank you so much."

"You're welcome", he said and left at that moment. Reia was upset because of Devansh's rude behaviour but then thought that he must have been gone through tough situations because of which he is behaving in this manner. She was about to leave when she saw a journal on a table. It was Devansh's.

FIVE

THE TRUTH UNTOLD

Reia was trying her best not to read Devansh's Journal. Constantly telling herself- "No this isn't the right thing to do, it is like invading someone's personal space. But this is where I can get all the answers, this is where I will get to know his story. She makes up her mind and opens to the very first page. 'It belongs to Devansh. R Shah', was written on the very first page.

'Dear diary it's May 28, today is the judgement day, today I'll know my true potential. Today I'll get to know if I make it in 'IEC'. May 29, I'm in I don't have words to describe my happiness, mom and dad are really happy. Now I'm waiting for the day when college starts.' After a few pages, she came upon the day when college started. 'June 10, it is finally the day when my new journey will begin. A clean slate, a new start to establish an identity, to find myself. June 11, IEC is huge and beyond my expectations, I made a lot of friends, everyone seems really nice, the professors are great, the seniors are supportive.

It's like I'm living a dream.'

"Reia come down fast for breakfast if you are ready or you'll get late for college", Reia's mom shouted from downstairs. "Coming", Reia replied. She kept the diary in her cupboard packed everything and went downstairs. After breakfast, she left for the college with Neha and Sanjana. Reia seemed lost in her thoughts, thinking about Devansh, what made him the monster that everyone says he is. Neha noticed Reia and asked, "Everything ok, R?" To which Reia nodded with a smile.

Reia was not able to focus on anything that day only thing bugging her was to know what happened. She spent the whole day looking at Devansh and thinking about him. Why did he do such a thing, or did he never do anything?

After the day concluded Reia was all alone going down to the parking lot when a senior guy named Aksh approached her. "So how was it to make love to four guys huh?" Everyone was watching. Reia ignored him and started walking fast when he chased her and obstructed her path.

"How you feel after realising that you've been used. Used as a toy by three others." Please leave me", pleaded Reia sobbing. "God they must've enjoyed every second of yours", said Aksh and the moment he uttered the last word, Devansh came running and knocked him down and sat on his chest and started punching him, hitting his face and shouting, " Why do you want to bother her. Why do you want to be a monster in someone's life? Why do you want to embarrass her in front of everyone."

At this time two professors came and lifted off Devansh and separated him from Aksh who was covered in blood rushing out of his nose. "The monster himself is speaking about doing good deeds. You know you did the same thing

they did. You are also a monster who feeds on a girl's body. Did you forget what you did with her?", Aksh screamed at Devansh. Devansh broke the moment he heard those words one can see that he was hurt just by looking at his face. One of the professors, Mr Ansh said, "Let's go to the Principal's office, shall we? And Mr Aksh you too, go wash your face and come to the Principal's office. Ms Reia you too please."
The whole scenario was told to the Principal and afterwards, she said, "Do you have anything to say, Mr Shah?" Devansh didn't answer. "So it concludes that Devansh and Aksh would e suspended for a month for college."

Reia was astonished about why didn't Devansh good the truth, why does he want to bare punishment for what he didn't do. So she interrupted Mrs Satyamurthy and said, "Ma'am Devansh is innocent he was helping me, he was defending me because Aksh was speaking ill things about and my character. He doesn't deserve the punishment." "If this is the case then I cancel your suspension but I have to give you detention for the violent action you took.

All of them left the Principal's office, Reia approached Devansh and said, "Why didn't you speak anything when the Principal was suspending you. You were innocent you didn't deserve to be punished." Devash retaliated, "I am not innocent, I'm a monster didn't you hear him? I deserve to be punished, I deserve to be tortured every day. So just leave me as I am and stay away from me cause I'm not the good guy", and then he left.

'June 28, today I met this girl named Naira, she is sweet, funny and damn beautiful. The moment saw her I felt something, she was wearing a pink dress and a hair tie holding her curls but not all, one or two curls escaped the tie and were whirling with

the wind playing on her face and obstructing the view of her deep blue eyes. Deep like an ocean in which I am willing to drown. She is a senior. I really want to get to know her better.

July 4, She was staring at me, she wasn't taking her eyes off me not even for a second and blushing and smiling at me. . I wonder if she likes me too. I think I am gonna ask her out. July 15, We have started to get along, we are spending a lot of time together and we are enjoying each other's company. July 18, I finally asked her out and she agreed to go on a date with me. The big day is on 22nd I'm taking her to the cafe 'Brewing Goodness'. July 25, I had my first kiss. It was amazing like I united with the missing part of my soul.

August 8, Everything is grand, I am enjoying college have a super cute senior girlfriend. Though we are not spending a lot of time together but still I love every second we are together.

August 15, Today I went to the library in my free time to read, I decided to read some classics so I went to pick up a book and I saw someone, it was Naira with a guy snuggling and kissing him. And when she saw me she just came to me and said, " Welcome to the dark side". I had my heart shattered into pieces. All the things we promised each other, all the dreams we dreamt together to achieve one day, everything was a lie.

August 21, Naira called me and asked me to meet after college as she wanted to talk to me. I forgot everything and decided to have a fresh start with her. It was 2 at the noon we decided to meet in the amphitheatre, she came ad told me that we are not going to work out and as she was leaving I just held her hand to tell her about how I felt, but the moment I touched she started screaming for help and started to hurt herself. I didn't know what was going on. In a few moments, I felt a hard hit on my back and I fell. A group of seniors started hitting me they were kicking me in my torso and they left me there with me whining in pain and while I was about to lose consciousness I saw Naira in the arms of the same guy with whom she was making out in the library.

August 25, I have sentenced to imprisonment for the next 13 years. Everyone is claiming me as a monster, my friends, the people I call family everyone. My dad in a traumatic breakdown, I lost my mother the moment she heard about the scenario her heart stopped beating right in front of me in my dad's arms. I have done that I am the reason for my mother's death. I really am a monster.

Reia was stunned and got into an emotional breakdown after reading the scenario she also notice some spots of teardrops that justify Devansh was crying while writing.

'Day 12, I don't know what kind of hell this is I spend my whole day in a room with only myself. Right at 4o' clock they bring me out of the cell and throw me on the ground where other prisoners beat me really hard. They say this is the way a molester should be treated, that I have to pay for the crime I committed. I am then thrown into the cell with my pain, blood gushing out wounded. Day 24, I haven't got food for 2 days now I'm starving.

Day 80, I don't know what is happening I remain blacked out the whole day I lay down after paying for my crimes at 4 and then wake up late at night when my body demands food but is not provided with. Day 234, I met dad today he didn't talk that much, he was just crying. That's all.

I don't know how many days have passed but the law decided to set me free and give me a chance to complete my education. My dad was happy that he gets to spend some time with me says life gave me a chance to live, but I think that it is just another torture to go in that with the tag of a molester and in a place where love destroys you completely.'

Reia felt really bad for Devansh and decided to help him. She knew that Devansh was put in a trap. She knew that he is innocent.

SIX

SALUD, NEW FRIEND

'Dear diary, I feel really bad for Devansh. He does not deserve the hate and the hardships he is going through. He deserves a happiness, love and friends and I am ging to help him get this all.'

Reia had decided to speak with Devansh today and also be friends with him. She reached the class and found Devansh sitting all alone by himself on the last bench. She approached him and sat beside him.

"Good Morning", said Reia with a cheerful smile but Devansh didn't respond. "I said good morning, Devansh". "I told you to stay away", glared Devansh. "And I choose not to. Instead I want to know you, I want us to be friends", Reia back-answered him. "Whatever", said Devansh and the class began.

After the lecture Devansh moved out of the class, Reia followed him, despite she knew she was banking her lectures she followed him. After a few steps, Devansh noticed that Reia was following him like his tail. He turned back and shouted, "Why are you following me. Stop bugging me." She just passed him a smile. Devansh then hurried to his car and left.

Reia was in utter disappointment she wanted to help Devansh but just couldn't. She knew it was a tough job but there was going back now. She tried to talk to him for days now but he always ignored her. Then came the day when Reia decided that she won't be leaving without speaking with Devansh today. The class got over and she hurried behind him, Neha saw her leaving, she waved at her but Reia didn't notice her.

She swiftly came in his way and stopped him from going ahead and raged at him, "What is your deal huh? Are you playing hard to get? If someone is being nice to you then you should be nice too. Just look at yourself your life is a mess, you are a loner, with no friends, no one to speak to. I'm trying so hard to be friends with you but you are just humiliating me. "I told you to stay away from me, I'm the bad guy of everyone's story. I will hurt you", said Devansh and walked away. She spoke with her back facing his, "No you are not. You are not a bad guy, you are just a misunderstood person. The guy who was forced by the world to change."

Devansh stopped the moment he heard those words. Reia continued, "I know what all has happened, actually I read your diary, I found it in the library. And from what I read you are not the villain of this story. You are the victim, who is broken and tortured who doesn't want anything but love and warmth. I understand your pain." Reia turned holding his diary in her hand. "So would you give me a chance? Our friendship a chance?" Devansh turned around and took the diary and left.

Reia was disappointed she knew that she did all she can but in vain. She was returning back to college when a car came honking at her. When she looked back it was Devansh peeping from the window. He asked Reia with his usual straight face, "Are you coming?" "Where?", asked Reia. "Don't you trust your friend?" Reia smiled and got into the car. Neha saw Reia getting into the car she called her but by then they left.

Reia saw a copy of 'To kill a Mockingbird " on the dashboard. "You read?", she asked. " Yes, books are the only thing that gives me it's all without any judgement. And besides, I can relate a lot with Tom Robinson (a reference to the story of 'To kill a Mockingbird')."

Reia nodded in agreement. After travelling for a while the car stopped, they both got out of the car. They came on top of a nearby mountain. Reia was stunned by the beautiful visual of the city as the sun was setting and the city was about to get lit by the artificial lights. Birds flying in-group towards their nest, people returning to their homes after a long tiring day.

"Isn't it beautiful?", asked Devansh. "Yes it is", Reia replied. "This is my favourite place to visit you know I come here whenever I feel low, whenever I want to escape the cruel world down there and find some peace. I stay here till the stars appear and then I speak with the person I love the most in the world, my mother.

My dad told me that the afterlife is within the stars, there is never and oblivion." Reia was just gazing at Devansh who was displaying a rare moment of smiling. They both sat down on the ground and were looking at the night sky.

It was 7 in the evening and Reia hadn't returned from college. Mrs Sharma called Neha if Reia was with her. Neha said, "No aunty, in fact, she wasn't with me on the way home. She went with someone, I thought it was her father." "No her father didn't go to pick her up and her phone is switched off too", said Reia's mother. Neha reached Reia's home as soon as she can.

"How are you mom? I'm fine I miss you tho", Devansh started speaking looking up at the stars. "Dad is also doing well, he misses you too he doesn't show it but I know he does.

And I'm not alone at the college anymore, see this a new friend I made", he spoke looking towards Reia who had a smile on her face and then he again looked up. "Her name is Reia". Reia looked at her watch it was 7:30 she said to Devansh, "Hey it's 7:30." "Bye ma it's getting late I'll speak with you later", said Devansh and left.

"Aunty, on my way here I contacted a few friends to ask them if Reia was with them. She isn't with any of our friends but one guy said that he saw Reia with Devansh. And he is not a good guy". Mrs Sharma was terrified. She left the house with Neha to get t the nearest police station, to file a complaint. And as she was leaving a black wagon came to their doorstep and Reia came out of the car. Reia's mother was happy to see her daughter safe she hugged her and asked, "Where were you?" And what happened to your phone?" "Battery died. Sorry mom but I was with Devansh", said Reia pointing towards him. "Thank you Devansh for giving her a ride home", said Reia's mother and then Devansh left.

Neha bursted with anger on Reia, "Don't you know he is a criminal. Are you out of your mind Reia? How can you go with him?" "No he is not a criminal", said Reia and told everything about the diary to Neha and Reia's mother. "How do you know it's true and it is not something he made up?", asked Reia's mother. " I trust him, Mumma. He is a nice guy who is just masked by the people, categorised as a criminal. And in fact, he was the one who saved me that night. Please let's give him a chance. Neha and Mrs Sharma nodded in agreement but deep down were worried about Reia's friendship with Devansh.

The next morning the one at Reia's house rung and an officer informed that Om and the other four guys are caught and legal action will be taken. After this news, Reia's dad made sure that they get the punishment they deserved.

SEVEN

A Feeling Like Never Felt Before

'Dear diary, the friendship between me and Devansh has deepened, we hang out every day after college. Even Neha, Dhruv and Sana have welcomed him into our circle. He seems very happy. He is smiling again and I am happy knowing that I am the reason behind his smile.'

'Dear diary, I'm feeling alive again, no more depression, no more sadness only happiness around me. All of this is because of the entry of a good friend into my life. Her name is Reia, she is sweet and kind. We spend a lot of time talking with each other and while talking with her I feel she really understands the pain and hardships I've been through. But I am scared, scared that this will end one day, scared that there will be an end to my happiness, scared that the end is near.'

It was Friday, the last working day of college for the week. Everyone gathered in the Physics laboratory for the practical class. Pairs were made so that two people can work on the experiment. Neha was paired with Aditya, Dhruv with Sana, Reia with Devansh and so on.

They began the practical, everyone working as a unit. Everyone helping each other. Devansh and Reia we're studying diodes and carrying out the experiments. Reia stretched her hands to take the Multimeter at the same time as Devansh was lifting it, their hands touched each other.

They felt each other before by this time it was different, there was a different spark, a different intensity was felt. Reia quickly backed off and let Devansh pick up the multimeter.

Everyone was done with their practicals. The next lecture was cancelled as the professor was on leave. Reia decided to hang out at the cafeteria, she decided to g to the cafe after a very long time. Neha refused the idea saying, "I have a meeting to attend, the cultural fest is coming soon and we have to start the preparation. So sorry but you all can carry on." Sana added, "Sorry Reia but I am also going out with Dhruv you can join us if you want". "No no you guys carry on. I'll hang out with Devansh". Everyone parted. Reia went to Devansh who was packing his bag.

"Let's go to the cafe.", Reia said. "Sure", he replied and followed Reia. They went and sat at a table for two. Reia ordered two lattes for them.

They started to interact. "So Devansh, what are your plans after college?", asked Reia. Devansh replied, "Well if I really get a life after college I want to become a published author". "You write?", Reia asked. "Yes I love to. I have written some poems", Devansh replied. Reia requested, "Recite me one please." Devansh declined the thought. But Reia pleaded repeatedly, "Please Dev, please for me." "Ok, ok here it goes. It is called 'The Night Of Intimacy'-

We got this king size to ourselves,
Decorated with petals all over the place,
I wanna use my teeth to untie your lace.
I want your lips to undress me.
I want to get hooked on your tongue,
And kiss you till the last pocket of air in my lung.
Our naked bodies touching each other,
I want to tickle yours with a feather.
Tonight we make love,
With me lying down and you above.
I'm seeing your pain, seeing your pleasure,
Believe me, girl, your body is a treasure.
I'll make your wildest dreams come true,
You will be screaming 'I love you.'
This night you will never forget,
A high you will not regret,
This night full of love and intimacy.

'That was great", said Reia, "the description of love, the sexual tension between them is amazing. You have a great future as a writer, Devansh." "Now don't flatter me." They both busted into laughter. Reia asked Devansh, "Why do you always wear black and dark clothes? You should also try pastels. You'll look great." "I don't know I just love to wear black. All the clothes I own are black ad mostly dark shades of grey", said Devansh. "Are you kidding? Then we should go shopping immediately. Come on let's hurry", said Reia and took Devansh's hand and pulled him on the way out.

They both sat in Devansh's car with Reia in the driver's seat. They reached Greenwood Mall and went to a clothing store. Reia picked some clothes for him, a pastel pink tee a sky blue button-down and to add to his masculinity ripped denim. She handed the outfit to Devansh and asked him to try it out.

He went into the changing room to change. He wore the outfit and came out. He coughed to get Reia's attention. She looked at Devansh the blue shirt complementing his dark skin and directing all focus to his mesmerising hazel eyes. "You are looking great Devansh", said Reia and clicked a picture of Devansh " try those too", she pointed to another few clothes she picked out.

He tried all one by one and they were done.

He went into the room to change into his old clothes. He called Reia to hand him his shirt which he forgot on the couch Reia came to give it. He opened the door a bit. A small door opening giving glimpses of his divine body, looked like God his sculpted it himself. His back left Reia breathless.

The scars he got in the prison were visible, they were looking like some tattoos. He turned and started buttoning his shirt starting from the sculpted chest to down to his abs which were in perfect symmetry. The drop of sweat slid down from his chest going through each muscle and going down to meet his belly button. This scenario fastened Reia's heartbeat she couldn't think anything but can only picture Devansh's naked body with 'The Night Of Intimacy' playing on loop in her head.

She couldn't get Devansh's picture out of the mind while eating, speaking even in bed before sleepin, all could she see are the glimpses of Devansh's perfect naked body.

EIGHT
Love Realised

'Dear diary, something happened yesterday. Yesterday I felt different around him. Yesterday I was seeing Devansh in a way I never saw, I could see his dreamy eyes, his charming smile and his hot body. I don't know why but all of a sudden I feel attracted to him. But I don't think that this can happen. It feels forbidden.'

It was Saturday morning, Reia woke up and got ready. Devansh was going to come over to work on a project for their Electronics class. It was around 1:15 in the afternoon when the doorbell rang. Reia opened the door. Devansh was standing on the doorstep hiding behind a huge pile of all the necessary things for the project. "Let me help you with that", said Reia taking a few things from Devansh. Their hand touched a bit, Reia felt it again, the feeling she never felt around him. They kept the things upstairs in Reia's room.

Reia looked at Devansh, who was looking like a delicacy in the panel pink tee that Reia picked for him. His toned muscular arms peeping out of the sleeves and a sight of his chest can be seen through the collar and those collar bones were making it hard for Reia to be around him. "You are looking beautiful Reia", said Devansh.

"What really? It's the first time he complimented me on my beauty", Reia spoke to herself. "Thank you and you too are looking like a snack I want to feed on". Reia said to Devansh. "Oops what did I just uttered? I'm a fool, what he must be thinking?", again Reia spoke to herself and then started laughing awkwardly and then was joined by Devansh's giggle.

" Let's begin", said Devansh. "Yeah sure", Reia replied. They started working. They were making a working electronic hydraulic hand. Devansh started with the project while Reia gazed at his handsomeness, appreciating his perfectly chiselled face and his messy long hair and falling for his eyes and the luscious and kissable red lips.

After a while, they took a break from their work and went downstairs for a snack. They both sat at the dining table and Reia's mother served them pancakes. Devansh took a bite and his eyes became moist. "What's the matter Devansh? Are you okay child?", asked Reia's mother. Devansh put a smile on his face to hide the tears and said, "It's nothing. Just that it's been a long time since I ate a meal that is filled with a mother's love." Reia's mother hugged Devansh tightly and said, "Don't worry child I'm like your mother too. Come here anytime whenever you feel like having a meal filled with motherly love".

After they finish eating they headed to Reia's room to continue the project. On their way up Reia's mom said, "Darling I'll be leaving for the market shortly so just watch over the house". "Yes mom", said Reia. She entered her room and saw Devansh holding her copy of 'To kill a Mockingbird". "You started reading To Kill a Mockingbird?", asked Devansh to which Reia replied, "Yes because it is something you relate to and I also wanted to relate to it." Devansh looked at Reia with a broad smile clearly reflecting love and admiration for Reia.

Reia turned on the music player, Party till Night, by L&H started playing. She took Devansh's hand and started to groove on the beats. "Come on let's dance and unwind", she said. They danced the shit out and enjoyed it a lot. Both of them tired lay down on Reia's bed, both close to each other. Devansh's hand landed on Reia's hand, her heart pounded like hell the sensual sound of Devansh's deep breaths was arousing her. She immediately stood up and said, " Let's begin with the project." "Yeah sure", replied Devansh and stood up.

An hour or two passed they were almost done. Devansh was standing stretching his body upwards and working on the fittings. Both of his arms upwards, pulling up the shirt and revealing his waist. Reia was trying hard not to fall for him. Devansh shouted in pain Reia immediately came back to reality and looked at what happened to Devansh. His hand was bleeding, blood gushing out. "What happened Devansh?", asked Reia. "It's a minor cut I'll be alright", answered Devansh. Reia shouted at him, "Are you mad. We have to dress this wound come with me."

Reia took out the first aid kit and started applying the antiseptic and softly blowing wind to soothe the wound and then she dressed his hand and was holding it. Devansh was watching Reia, her concern for him. They both were close their legs touching each other and both lost in each other's eyes. Reia got close to him when Devansh backed off, stood up and turned away removing his hand from Reia's.

"What's wrong Devansh. Are you mad?", asked Reia. Devansh was quiet. "Say something Devansh! Don't you like me?", asked Reia. "You are a nice girl Reia and really beautiful", said Devansh. Reia asked, "Then why do you keep running away from me. Tell, me tell..." "Because I am scared that I will fall in love with you if I kiss you. Then I won't be able to help myself but I will be utterly consumed by you and your love."

Reia pulled him close and whispered in his ears, "KISS ME Then". She reached to his neck and got on her tiptoes and Devansh, holding her waist brought her close, so close that they can hear each other's heart beating fast and the warmth of each other's deep breath. They closed their eyes his parted lips met her, love was felt and feelings were shared. Both were getting breathless in a way they were enjoying.

Reia reached his sort buttons and started to unbutton his shirt and whispered in the most sensual way that Devansh had ever heard, "I want you". She pushed him onto the bed and removed her top. Both kissing each other passionately and their naked bodies touching each other. He was seeing the pain hidden by the pleasure. He went on slow on a high tempo and whispered "I am so lucky to love you" and he kissed her while listening to her holy moans. They both laid down with Reia's head on his chest enjoying the sound of his heartbeat. And then looked at Devansh with a smile and reached his lips to kiss and then Devansh kissed her forehead.

NINE

LOVE UNDER STARS

'Dear diary, finally I feel like my life is not miserable as I used to think it is. Alas after so many hardships I finally found my happy place, I finally found the person who makes me feel like she is the part that completes my soul. I just can't imagine a day without Reia. Before she came I thought it was cliche but talking to you feels like praying to God, though I don't believe in Almighty but both the feelings are equally divine. Now I pray to God everyday because of you. Tell him to not to put an end to us. After so many years I finally feel like to stay alive, to live just to see her, talk to her and to be around her. I don't want to die, at least not now.'

"Devansh I hope you informed Reia about tomorrow's dinner", asked Mr Shah. "Yes dad I told her and she is going to come by 8", replied Devansh. "Great. I'll make her my special Paneer Tikka and Yakhani Pulao", said Mr Shah. Devansh was looking at his dad all excited to welcome his son's girlfriend.

'Dear diary, tomorrow is a big day for me tomorrow I am going to meet Devansh's dad. I hope all of it goes well. Honestly speaking, I am nervous for tomorrow, will his dad like me? What if he is an angry nature. I just hope that tomorrow goes well. And a good news I got today is that Om and the other culprits got the punishment they deserve. They have been imprisoned for 5 years and turns out they were also in the influence of drugs. Turns out that Om has a very dark past which he sugarcoats with all the cliche and simp behaviour.'

It was 7 in the evening Devansh came to pick up Reia. He approached the door and knocked the door. Reia opened the door wearing a Red salwar and kurti that perfectly fit her body, defining her curves thee, red lipstick forcing Devansh to kiss her. Her delicate hands decorated with golden bangles and her ears with cute little earrings.The small bindi on her forehead making him fall for her all over again, her luscious long hair playing with the wind. She was looking like incarnation of goddess Lakshmi (Hindu Goddess of Beauty).

Devansh got lost in Reia's beauty. He was just standing their gazing at her. Three minutes passed but still Devansh hadn't took his eyes from Reia. "Let's go Dev", said Reia but Devansh gave no response. " Dev.. Devansh....hello let's go", Reia repeated while shooting Devansh. Devansh escaped the hypnotic effect of Reia's beauty and returned back to reality. "I have something for you can you just turn around?", he said. Reia turned around and Devansh took out a necklace from his pocket and tied it around her neck. It was Reia's grandma's necklace. "Oh Dev, where did you get this ?" After that day I found it on the ground in the parking lot, broken. So I kept it with me and I gave it to jeweller to repair and I just got it back yesterday", said Devansh. "Oh Devansh, it really means a lot to me. This necklace is the last thing that my grandma left for me. I'm really thankful to you. I love you", she said and they started walking. As they were walking Reia said, "What happened why did you froze like a computer back there?"

"Nothing", said Devansh. "Actually, I got mesmerised by your beauty. Your beauty left me speechless", said Devansh and kissed Reia and then handed her the roses he brought for her. Reia blushed and sat in the car.

Devansh stopped the car got down quickly and rushed to the other side and opened door for Reia, bowed and said, "Please my lady" and offered his hand. Reia took his hand and got down and kissed Devansh's cheek. "What was this for?", he asked. "Should there be a reason to kiss my boyfriend?", asked Reia. "So my question is answered with another question", said Devansh smiling and brought Reia closer and gave her a kiss on her lips.

Then they moved towards Devansh's home. It was a two storey bungalow beautifully lit by lights as if it was some festival. They approached the door and rung the doorbell. Reia was a bit nervous, she started taking deep breaths. Devansh noticed her and whispered, "Don't worry babe, everything will go well."

Then Devansh's dad opened door, a tall man with some patches of grey hair wearing a red shirt with black trousers was standing in front.

He looked tough and strict but the pleasing smile on his face really changed ones opinion. "Welcome Reia, welcome to Shah Villa. It's not huge but it is our home". Reia entered and replied, "It is beautiful sir, really." "Don't say sir, child, you can call me uncle if you want it feels more close", said Mr Shah. "Yes uncle".

"Come have a seat", said Mr Shah and sat down on the couch. Devansh poured some water in a glass and offered Reia. She took it with a smile and drank it. "Oh so you can offer water to a girl but not do even a single chore for dad huh?", said Devansh's dad sarcastically. "Dad!" Devansh exclaimed. His dad replied laughing, "I'm kidding he really helps me out with everything. I am happy to have him as my son. He is a clear reflection of his mother, he makes me feel like she is with me till this date, everyday" and took Devansh close.

"Dad, I'll just give a home your to Reia, what you say?", Devansh asked. "Yes sure but first let's eat or the food will get cold and all my hard work will go in vain", said Mr Shah. "You cooked the food, uncle?", asked Reia. "Yes but don't be scared he is a really good chef. I eat his cooked food everyday and you see me healthy and fit everyday", said Devansh giggling and the room busted in laughter.

They all sat on the dinner table, and prayed to God, thanked for the food. They began to eat. Mr Shah eagerly waiting for Reia's review on the food. She took the first bite and closed her eyes lost in the flavour of the food. "It's amazing. Uncle you are great chef! Better than my mom." His dad replied, "Thank you". And Devansh teased Reia, "I am going to tell aunty what you just said". Reia hit him on the arm and started laughing.

Mr Shah was making sure that Reia are without hesitation and whole heartedly. He was forcing her to eat more. At last Reia took the last bite of the Yakhani Pulao and said, "I am done uncle, please no more." And stood up to wash her hands.

Then Devansh told his dad, "I am going to show Reia around". "Yes ok", said his Dad.

They began the tour with the living room. "This is the living room, we father and son hang out here and also talk about mom sometimes", said Devansh. "Is that your mom, Devansh?", asked Reia pointing at the photo hung on the wall behind the TV. He replied, "Yes, she sits there and observe if we are keeping her home nice and tidy." "She was so beautiful", said Reia. "Yeah she was", said Devansh with his eyes moist. Reia took him close to her and said, "I am sorry for your loss, it will be okay."

Then he showed her his parents room and then proceeded to his room. He said "And this a my kingdom. Or I should say our future kingdom." Reia blushed. "This the table where we will work, this is the bathroom where we will bathe together and this is the bed where we will...." Reia put her finger on his lips telling him to stop and started blushing.

She was looking around when she came across a trophy exhibit. She asked him, "You won all these trophies?". "Yes, before I was put behind bars I used to play basketball. But then everything changed after that day."

"Come I want to show you something", said Devansh and took Reia's hand and moved. They went up to their terrace and on their and closed Reia's eyes with his eyes. "Where are you taking me?", asked Reia. "We are almost there babe", said Devansh and took his hands off her eyes and Reia opened her eyes and saw the sky full of bright twinkling stars. "It is beautiful!", she exclaimed.

They sat down looking at the stars with Reia leaning her head on Devansh's shoulder. "I love this", said Devansh "I don't want this to end." Reia said, "It won't I promise. I love you till my last breath." "And what if I took the last breath before you? Will you still love me?", asked Devansh. "Don't say such things Devansh. I'll love you no matter what and this is a promise.

Devansh looked at Reia with a smile. Reia came closer and kissed him. Devansh holding her passionately slid his hand down near her breast and kissed her neck. She pulled him down and kissed him passionately, his neck, his lips, his chest and undressed him with her lips. He gave her all the heavenly pleasures. He pentrated her with passion making her feel special, making her feel divine, making her feel like her pleasure is his utmost priority.

Her heart beating faster, deep breaths and her heavenly moans showing how much she was loving him

TEN

TABLES TURNED.

It was September 8, Final examinations were about to get over. The final bell rung students started coming out of the examination hall. There was chaos everywhere, some students discussing the question paper while some having fun even in the tensest atmosphere.

Devansh came from behind and put his arm around Reia who was walking at a distance from him. He asked, "Hey babe, how was the exam?" Reia replied, "Great, what about you?" "It was okay", he said "I hate Mathematics you know right. I'll manage not to fail tho."

After walking a few steps he continued, "Listen I am planning to go on a trip to Ladakh after the examinations. What do you say? Just you and me on a bike exploring the scenic beauty." "That's great but I have to ask Mumma and Papa...", she was speaking but was interrupted by Devansh, " I'll speak with Mom if you want." Reia replied, "No I'll speak with her today and inform you about it." "Ok", he said and then they both got in the car and headed to Reia's home to drop her off.

Reia spent the whole evening gathering courage to speak with her parents. She really wanted to go to Ladakh with Devansh.
It was 8 the whole family gathered for dinner. Reia was a bit nervous to speak anything. There was a dreading silence around the table. Her father broke the silence and asked, "So Reia how are your exams going on?" She answered, "Great dad. I promise I'll excel in all the examinations." "Yeah I know baby girl. You will excel", her dad said.

After staying quiet for a while she spoke, "Mum, dad I want your permission for something, I want to go on a trip to Ladakh with Dev after exams, he is been planning it ." "Yeah sure", said her dad and Mom continued, "You may." "Please Mumma, please papa I really wanna go... Wait what. Did you just give me permission for the trip?", asked Reia. "Yeah, we did. Devansh is a good kid and you all have been studying hard, you deserve a small trip. Enjoy but safely", said her dad. She stood up excited and hugged her mom and dad and said, " Thank you, thank you so so much. I love you guys. I'll just inform Dev right now". "Hey first finish your dinner, Reia!!!", yelled her mother but the so excited Reia had gone by now.

She went to her room picked up her phone and called Devansh, "Hey Dev, Ladakh is on!!" He replied, "Oh yeah I was a bit scared cause I did all the bookings prior and the fees were not refundable. But I am happy. Ladakh we are coming. We will leave after three days ok?" Great, can't wait for it. See you tomorrow, love you", she said. He replied, "Love you too babe."

September 10, the final bell rang, an excited mob of students came out of the examination Hall, everyone gay. All were excited, no one cared about the paper if it was easy or tough, and all were happy about the vacations that were about to begin. Devansh came out of the examination hall looking for Reia. Reia was standing at a distance with Neha and Sana looking for Devansh. Devansh ran towards Reia and hugged her and lifted her in his arms, Reia leaned forward and kissed him. Neha exclaimed, "Oh my God! you guys, get yourself a room".

Reia went with Devansh to his home after the exam to spend some time with him. They both went to his room where Devansh showed her all the preparations he did for the trip. He was playing around with his camera and Reia was picking clothes for him to wear standing by the wardrobe.

"Hey Reia give me a pose", he said pointing the camera towards Reia. Reia made some funny faces, funny but cute. He clicked some pictures and giggled and said, "Hey look you are looking so cute, I am going to frame these pictures." Reia came and saw the pictures and tried to snatch the camera and said, "No delete those, I am looking stupid in these pictures, give me the camera I want to delete those." Devansh started running and said, "You are looking cute in these I am not gonna let you delete these. Catch me if you can", Reia started chasing him. She said in a bit louder voice while running, " Dev please delete those, d you want to make me cry?" "Yes", he replied and rushed downstairs with Reia chasing him.

They went to and fro through all the rooms, then dodging around the dining table in the kitchen, running all around the house. After a while, Dev slowed down and Reia caught him and they both laid down on the couch in the living room. Both of them breathing heavily and they looked at each other and started laughing. They both were drowning in the depths of each other's eyes.

Reia immediately got on top of Devansh, sitting on his lap with her leg around him facing him and admiring his beauty. She took off her top and grabbed his neck and kissed him. Starting from his forehead then down to his nose to his lips. Then she kissed passionately his lips and bit his ear and whispered, "Give it to me Dev. Fuck me until you can".

Then she took off his shirt and kissed him down the neck to the chest and met his belly button and went down. She pushed him down on the couch and then rode him with passion, giving him all heavenly experience. "I love you", he said "I love you too", she replied as they both reached climax together. What they started together, ended together with Reia sleeping with her head on Devansh's muscular, bare chest with his hands around him.

It was 11:30 at the night, Reia was in her bed asleep when her phone rang. She woke up, turned on the lights and answered the phone, it was Devansh, scared and sobbing. "Help me Reia, they are here to take me back. Come and save me I don't want to go. I'm scared, please come fast. Please Reia help me." "What happened Devansh are you ok babe?", asked Reia. "I don't want to go. They are here please come and help me....."

ELEVEN

LIFE ISN'T FICTION.

'Dear diary, today I realised something, that life is never perfect. The world can never see you happy, life is not a movie it's reality, and not every story ends happily. Some stories are written to reflect sadness, with the motive of shattering the dreams of the main character. In my case, it's my story and I am the main character. Yesterday the police came and took Dev to prison. The court reopened his case due to political pressure and has set him on trial by the word of Naira and her family. The decision will be taken in the coming two days, dad has taken over Devansh's case and is trying his best to save him.'

It was September 12, and the court adjusted still no decision was taken tomorrow was the final day of the decision. Tomorrow was going to decide the future of Devansh and Reia, whether they would be able to spend their lives together or will Devansh be sentenced to imprisonment for 10 years.

Reia came to meet Devansh at the prison. They both were going to meet in a small room with a huge glass between them. The glass is the barrier between them, not letting them meet each other, hug each other or love each other. Reia sat on the chair and waited for Devansh. After a while, Devansh entered limping his face bruised and bleeding showing that he was beaten up by his fellow cellmates. Reia saw him entering and was trying hard to hold back her tears. Devansh came and sat down slowly his bruised body making it hard for him to sit down. Then they both picked up the telephone to speak with each other.

Reia asked trying hard not to sound sad, "How are you, babe?" "I was a bit sad and hurt but listening to your voice aided all my wounds, all menta and physically", he replied. These words brought tears to her eyes and she raised her hand and touched the glass and then Devansh touched her hand but still the glass not allowing them to feel each other.

"You hate me don't you?", asked Devansh. "No, I love you and will still love you no matter what the situation is. I will never stop loving you" said Reia sobbing. "You know I saw a dream. A dream that I become a successful author who writes our love story, our eternal love story. But now Iit will never come true", said Devansh. "Why are you always so negative Devansh?", asked Reia. Devansh replied, "What if I am sentenced to 10 years of imprisonment?" "You will not and even if it happens so you will have a life after that, a life where you are an author and a life where you have me. I am willing to wait for 100 years for your love how hard is it to wait for 10?"

A police officer came and pulled away Devansh from the table and was taking him back to his cell. "No please let me speak for a few minutes more", he request as he was struggling to take Reia's hand through the glass.

It was September 13, the day of judgement. All of Devansh's friends including Reia, Sana, Neha and Dhruv we're present. Reia's family and Devansh's dad were also in the court hoping for the case to conclude in Devansh's favour.

The court was called in order Naira's lawyer began by saying, "My lord the culprit should be given a punishment for 10 years as he sexually assaulted my client, Ms Naira Kapoor. I have presented all the proofs that are all against him." The case was taken forward with a lot of arguments, and a lot of insults were made at Devansh's character and his parenting.

Devansh was looking hopeless as if he had already lost the case. He was broken, broken by the cruel words he was hearing about him and his parents. Ill words about his mother who was no more, all the pain he was hiding behind his old straight face. Reia was trying so hard not to cry. Because she knew that because of her Devansh was playing strong.

Finally, it was time for the decision and the judge said, "The decision is taken in favour of Ms Naira Kapoor. Mr Devansh Shah has been sentenced to imprisonment for 10 years according to Section 354 IPC.

Everyone went into mental trauma. Devansh's dad was playing brave and telling his son to stay strong too. Reia could not hold back anymore. She ran towards Devansh and held his hand sobbing not letting the officers take him away from her. Neha and Reia's parents were holding her back.

'Dear diary it's been two days since Devansh has been imprisoned. I know that there will be a time when he will come back when he will be mine and only mine.'

September 20, Reia's home telephone rang, her mom picked it up and spoke with someone. After a while, she called Reia and hugged her right and said, "Reia it was Devansh's dad's call he was crying a lot. I think we should go to see him." "Why mom what happened?", asked Reia. "Now Reia I am going to tell you something but promise me you will stay strong", said her mother. "Yes mom, Devansh was hanged yesterday in the prison because of the pressure from Naira's family." Reia stood there with grief on her face no emotions, no sadness nothing.

It was two days since Devansh had passed away today was his final ritual. Reia and her family got ready and left for the ceremony. Reia hadn't cried since that day. She never expressed her sadness. She wasn't eating, she was not speaking, she was hurting herself. After the final rituals, Mr Shah was pouring Devansh's relations in the river and Reia was standing there all alone with a straight face watching her love go away from her far far away. She knew he was never going to come back.

Mr Shah took Reia close to him and said, "Do you miss him?" Reia nodded. "He loved you a lot. "He wanted you to be happy. It will hurt him to see that you are making yourself suffer. I also miss him. My life is misery but I decided to live happily for him and his mother. Because they want me to be happy. Here is a letter that Dev wrote for you before he was hanged. The officer gave it to me yesterday", said Mr Sharma and handed her the letter.

Reia hadn't opened the letter till now. She knew the moment she opened the letter she is going to break down. Neha came over that day to speak with Reia. She took the letter and read it aloud so that Reia can listen.

'Hey love, hope you are doing well. Well, I am feeling epic today even though in a few minutes a rope is going to break my neck and kill me but still, I don't regret it. The time that I spent with you has been the best time of my life. Your love is the reason that today I am going smiling at my death note. You know once I said that love is fictional only found in novels, you

proved me wrong. I realised that love is true when I found my Elizabeth Bennet, until I found the one who utterly consumed me and loved me as if I am the only one who she cared of. So thank you for proving me wrong and loving me. I am always grateful for that. Once someone asked me who do you love the most? And I answered myself. But today the police officer asked me the same question I replied a crazy, cute and a very special girl who is a short stack of pancakes, my stack, her name is Reia.

I want you to live a happy life after my death. Go crazy and live a life for yourself and me too. Go chase your dreams. Promise me and if you not I will always think that I was responsible for your misery. I know that you are going to cry today but I want you to smile tomorrow. Don't cry because I'm gone but smile because I was there, in fact, I am going to be there with you looking over you in my afterlife. I am also gonna meet mom after so long. Until next life. Love Devansh.'

Reia bursted into tears all the sadness, the trauma she carried with her which she buried deep in her finally came out. She was crying relentlessly. Neha hugged her and was patting and rubbed her back signifying that she is there for Reia.

TWELVE

ALWAYS AND FOREVER.

The event was final, thousands of people were gathered in Mariana hall. The stage was all set, the lights added to the ambience of the room. There was a chair at the centre of the stage with a confident woman sitting on it, wearing a black dress and narrating a story. It was Reia, everyone gathered for her book release named 'The Forbidden Story'. Thousands of people came to meet her, to hear her out.

She continued in a confident voice, "On this very day, six years ago, an innocent was hanged up to death. He was an ordinary guy like you all. A boy who was a dream, a dream of becoming an author someday, he saw a future with a girl. But all his dreams were shattered, and all his dreams were choked along with him. He never got to be an author because this cruel world never allowed him to. This innocent's story was trapped in his diary for years, his voice screaming for justice but was suppressed by the people.

This is not a story like other stories, where there is a happy ending. It is a story of grief, pain and sadness. But everyone should listen to it cause it shows how cruel this world has become. in today's world, you have to be selfish. Being selfless is a flaw, a weakness today. If you help someone give him all your love and warmth but still in future he will be the reason for your downfall, he will be the one who will betray you, who will break you down. Not every story ends with the victory of good over bad.

In some stories, evil defeat good. In fact, in this story, the villain is so powerful that our hero can't even fight against him. In fact, in some stories, a hero dies a heroic death, where the whole country is in grief and he is respected by all. But our hero didn't even get a heroic death, instead, he was portrayed as a monster who was killed for the betterment of all. Our hero just wants the world to know that he is not a villain, not even the hero but a good guy who became the victim.

Not every love story ends with the girl sleeping in the guy's arms. In this story, the guy sleeps in the girl's arms, but here he is never gonna wake up, he is gone far far away from her. So this is a different kind of story that demands to be listened to. In this way you can hear his side of the story, why he does not deserves the hate he got and why he is not the villain of the story, not even a hero but just an innocent who was murdered by the law.

You know he once said that love is something fictional, only found in novels. But he was proved wrong but he never got to experience that because the world didn't allow him to. But I still love him and I know he loves me too, he is there with me every day with me looking at me from his afterlife. Yes, he believed that there is an afterlife and now I also believe that there is and he is watching me from there and that one day when death comes to me, our love story will end in the afterlife like others where the girl is in the guy's arms. That day he will be mine and only mine. And no earthly being or heavenly being can separate us."

A reporter stood up and asked Reia, "One last question ma'am, you are the one who wrote this book then why on the front cover of the book it is written as by 'Devansh Shah'? Reia replied with a tinge of smile on her face, "Because I never wrote this story, it was written years ago by him that was trapped in his diary, I was just the voice for his words. I am just a medium who brought the story in front of the world. So indeed the writer of this book is late Devansh Shah."

After a while Reia looked up as if she knew that Devansh was listening and said with tears in her eyes, "You know Devansh, I thought that every part or phase in my life is a new chapter, a new beginning, a new story and I never had a problem with that until I met you. I wished that this story of his to never end, that you and I will be eternal throughout the cold and the warm days, but life isn't a fairytale and sometimes you are Juliet and not Cinderella. Perhaps in another life, you won't be my Romeo but my Prince Charming and until the next life, I will love you always and forever."

The audience applauded and stood up in respect and condolences for Devansh. After the event concluded Reia went and touched the feet of Mr Shah who lived with Reia and her family after Devansh's death so that Reia could look after him like a daughter he never had. He hugged Reia tightly and said, "Thank you, my child, thank you so much for bringing Dev's real story in front of the world he will be very happy and proud today." Reia replied, "The truth always reveals itself Dad". Reia was still single not because she decided to but because she never found another man who could replace Devansh, who can give her even 1% of the love that Devansh gave her. Neha, Sana and Dhruv were also present at the event to celebrate the success of both of their friends one who wrote the story and the other who told the story for him.

Devansh wanted to be a writer and write a story about his love but in the end, his love became a writer and wrote his story and told it to the world.

'Dear diary, I think that Devansh finally found peace after the world saw that he never was the monster but was portrayed as one. Today he finally found the love and respect he deserves. And yes I still love him and will always and forever.'

Printed by Libri Plureos GmbH in Hamburg,
Germany